Yasmin's Box

John Prater

CAMBRIDGE
UNIVERSITY PRESS

Yasmin found a big box. It looked
old and dirty.

Inside, she found a dirty old
lamp. Yasmin began to wipe it clean.

The lamp began to smoke, and the smoke became a genie!

"You can have four wishes," said the genie.

"First," said Yasmin, "can I have a
little black cat?"

"Kazam!"

Yasmin was holding a big black rat.

"Sorry," said the genie. "Let's try again."

Next, Yasmin said, "Can I have a
spotty dog?"

"Kazam!"

Yasmin was holding a noisy frog.

"I'm so sorry," said the genie. "Let's try again."

Then Yasmin said, "Can I have some nice things to eat?"

"Kazam!"
Yasmin had great big feet.

"You always get it wrong," said Yasmin.
"Let *me* try."

"Kazam!"

Now Yasmin had a little black cat,
a spotty dog and nice things to eat.

The dog played with the cat. Yasmin
and the genie ate and ate.

Then the genie said goodbye to Yasmin.

Dad came in. He said, "Look what I've got for your room – a new lamp."